For more information contact:

Center Reach Communications
191 University Blvd #271
Denver CO 80206-4613
http://CenterReachCommunication.com

ISBN: 978-0-9841949-0-2

PRINTED IN THE UNITED STATES OF AMERICA

Library of Congress Control Number 2009908674

Along time ago there lived a boy named Henry. Henry lived in a castle high on a cliff in a town called Sagres in a country called Portugal.

Henry didn't have brothers or sisters and his castle was far away from the townspeople. He had butlers and cooks and servants and tutors but they couldn't be his friends, what with always reminding him to wipe his feet and read his lessons. So when he was very young, Henry decided that the ocean that washed up on the shores far below the castle would be his friend.

He loved the ocean.

Every day when he awoke, Henry would throw the windows of his room wide open and call out to his friend, "Bom dia, meu amigo!" which meant "Good morning, my friend!" in the way Henry spoke.

When the skies were sunny, the sea would call back, "SSSsscccuuuush, sssssscccuuush," which Henry knew meant "Good morning to you, my friend," in the way the sea spoke.

Some days, the ravens would join in the conversation. "Caaaawww, Caaawwww," the ravens would say, which, of course, meant "Good morning, my chatty friends," in the way the ravens spoke.

Bom dia, meu amigo!

When Henry joined his mom and dad, the king and queen, at breakfast, he would talk only of his friend the sea.

"Father," he would ask, "does the sea have other friends besides me?"

His father would answer, "Henry, the sea doesn't have any friends. It fights the fishermen with its waves, and pulls divers to its bottom."

Henry didn't believe his father. He knew that the sea spoke to him with its kind words every morning.

So Henry would ask his mom, "Mother, who does the sea love?"

And his mother would answer, "Henry, the ocean is just the ocean, it doesn't love anyone or anything."

Henry didn't believe his mother because he knew the sea loved him. He would hear it call to him even when the skies were gray. "CuuuishCuuuish!" it would say, and Henry knew that meant "I love you!" in the way the ocean spoke.

One morning when Henry was almost eight, the skies were very dark. The wind blew and rain beat on the windows, but he had to say good morning to his friend. So he threw open his windows and, though the rain wet his face, he greeted his best friend saying, "Bom dia, meu amigo!" and waited for his response.

"Kkkkkkkkruuuuuuuussshhhhhk!" said the ocean.

Henry had never heard his friend speak like this. He rushed down to breakfast, hoping his mother and father could help.

"Father," Henry said, when he arrived at the table, "I think my friend is lonely."

"Henry, what friend is this?"

"The SEA!" Henry responded. "Father, may we go and keep him company?"

"Of course not!" Henry's father responded. "The rain is coming down in sheets and you have your lessons to attend to."

Kkkkkkkkruuuuuuuusssshhhhhk!

Henry searched for his mother and found her instructing the cooks as they made breakfast.

"Mother!" he said. "Call a carriage, my friend is so lonely!"

"What friend is this?" his mother asked.

"The SEA!" Henry said.

"The ocean isn't lonely, Henry. And if you don't get out of this kitchen, you'll be hungry."

At breakfast, Henry couldn't eat a thing; he was so worried about his friend.

"Henry, eat your breakfast!" his mother said.

"Henry, you'll spend the whole day in your room if you don't get to eating," his father said.

Still, Henry couldn't eat.

"Henry, I won't see you today," his father said, "because you'll be spending the day in your room!"

Henry went to his room, but all he could hear was his friend calling out to him, "Kkkkkkkkkkruuuuuuuuussshhhhhk! Kkkkkkkkkkruuuuuuuuussshhhhhk!" over and over again.

Henry went to the window and tried to soothe his friend. "Não chores," he said to the sea, "Don't cry, my friend." But still the sea cried.

Henry threw himself across the bed, but still his friend cried. Henry covered his head with his pillows, but still the sea cried. Henry cried himself, but it just made his friend cry harder, "Kkkkkkkkruuuuuuuuussshhhhhk!" "Kkkkkkkkruuuuuuuuussshhhhhk!" "Kkkkkkkkruuuuuuuuussshhhhhk!"

Henry went to the window and looked out. The rain was pelting his friend's great back and he could smell his salty tears. His deep blue face had turned grey with terrible white waves.

Henry thought, What kind of friend am I?

Kkkkkkkkkruuuuuuuuuussshhhhhk!

13

So he gathered his warmest scarf and his thickest socks. He put on his heaviest coat and tied the collar tight. He slipped a second pair of pants over his pajamas and opened the door to his room. He peered out to the right, then the left. No one was in sight, so he plodded quietly down the back stairs, barely taking a breath. Down the stairs, he peered again to the right, then to the left. No one in sight. He ran without breathing, out the servant's door.

The rain stung Henry's face and slipped down his neck.
He was cold, but his friend was crying louder now,
"Kkkkkkkkruuuuuuuussshhhhhk! "Henry ran down the cobbled road.
He ran and ran, ignoring his heavy coat and thick pants as they grew
soaked, forgetting about his cold hands and the rain seeping
down his neck.

As Henry ran, he cried out, "Não chores!" and "Aqui vou eu!"
"Don't cry, sea, here I come!" The sea only responded with more cries,
"Kkkkkkkkruuuuuuuussshhhhhk!" "Kkkkkkkkruuuuuuuussshhhhhk!"

Kkkkkkkkkruuuuuuuuussshhhhk!

Finally, Henry found his friend. Fishing boats littered his shores. On sunny days, Henry had seen the same boats – filled with fishermen and their dogs – glide along his friend's great back. He had watched as they went out to sea, keeping his friend company. He had watched them ready the nets and secure the oars. He had watched the dogs they took with them, dogs trained to herd the fish toward the boats. They dove and swam in the sea, sometimes diving deep underneath him.

This must be why he's so lonely, thought Henry. All his other friends are gone.

He called out, "I'm here!" But his friend cried so loudly that Henry couldn't even hear his own voice.

Henry stood calling to the sea, but he wouldn't stop crying. Henry didn't know what to do. He threw himself down on a rock.

Back at the castle, the queen had finished instructing the cooks on the lunchtime menu. Feeling bad for her son, she went up to his room. She knocked on the door, but no answer. "Henry!" she called. She opened the door. She saw his bed rumpled but no Henry. She searched his playroom and his lesson room. She called out again, "Henry!"

Henry, of course, was nowhere to be found.

The queen searched the castle for her husband. She found him in his study, reading.

"Husband," she said, "Henry is not in his room."

"Oh that boy!!" the king said. "Probably down with the cooks."

"I've just come from kitchen," said the queen.

"At the stables then."

"In this rain?"

"Send a butler to find him," said the king, "and stop worrying."

Meanwhile, Henry had his head braced on a rock, crying for both his friend and for himself. He was soaking wet and cold and nothing he could do would stop the crying.

Then, for a moment, he thought he heard his friend stop and he looked up. "Kkkkkkkkkkruuuuuuuuussshhhhhhk!!!" Another cry.

What am I going to do? Henry thought to himself.

Then he saw one of the boats move against the shore.

Henry wiped the rain and tears from his eyes. Hunched over the boat was a man in a wide-brimmed hat, with his overalls dripping from the rain. As Henry watched, the man stood, his wide chest facing the ocean. He raised his arm and a dog came running down the beach, brown and white with a curly coat which seemed dry despite the rain, ears flopping as she ran.

The dog jumped into the boat and seemed to bark, although Henry couldn't hear anything above his friend's crying.

Henry knew what to do. He wiped his tears on his heavy jacket and walked past the rocks, through the wet sand, to the man and his dog.

Kkkkkkkkkruuuuuuuuuussshhhhhk!

21

When Henry was close to the man, he cried out, "Please help my friend!"

The man turned, surprised. He thought he was the only one brave enough to weather the rough waters.

He was even more surprised to see the young boy, breathless and heavy with wet clothes. He can't be more than six years old, thought the fisherman, who the men called Diego Garcia.

"What's that you say?" yelled Diego. His voice was so deep Henry thought it might be the sea himself.

"I said, please help my friend!" Henry responded.

"What? Is someone hurt? Drowning?" Diego was annoyed, he was eager to get out to sea. His ancestors always said, "When it rains, fish." And he knew he'd pull in a great catch today.

"No, he's lonely," said Henry, now standing in front of the man. "Can't you hear him crying?"

"Can't hear anything over the crashing waves. But son, if your friend is out there," pointing out to sea, "no one can help him, not even me."

22

Just then the dog came bounding out of the boat.
"Aeaarff!" she said, which means "I'll help you!" in the way dogs talk.

"Her name is Milagro," said Diego. Henry knew that meant Miracle in the way fishermen talk.

"But I call her Millie. She nearly drowned as a pup and never grew to her full size. Most men thought she was too small for fishing but she comes from a royal line of dogs. She'll dive for nets my men could never recover and she'll swim in any weather. That's why I call her Miracle."

Henry rubbed Millie's fuzzy head. She could be his friend, he thought, but again he heard "Kkkkkkkruuuuuuuuussshhhhhk!"
and remembered his other friend, the sea.

Aeaarff!

"Sir," said Henry.

"Call me Diego," the man said.

"About my friend."

"Son, I told you, there's nothing we can do in these rough seas."

"But my friend IS the sea, Mr. Diego. He has been my friend since I was very young, my only friend, and I can't bear to hear him crying. He's lonely. I came here to keep him company."

"Boy, first of all the sea is not your friend, especially not today. And second, the sea is a she, not a he."

"Excuse me, Mr. Diego, but I think you are wrong. He is my friend, he says good morning to me every day."

"Son, the sea doesn't say good morning."

"Sure he does," said Henry. "He says, 'Sssscccuuuush, ssssscccuuuush,' which means good morning in the way seas talk. But for the last two days he has just cried."

Ssssscccuuuuuush

Just then the sea spoke again, "Kkkkkkkkruuuuuuuussshhhhhk!"

"See, that means he's lonely," said Henry.

"Son…"

Henry interrupted, "But if we could take your boat out, I'm sure he would stop crying. He just needs a little company."

Diego was eager to take his boat out, but not to calm the seas. He wanted to fish. He looked at the boy. He was too small and weak to man the heavy nets. Besides, he'd never seen the boy on a boat before, he was sure he couldn't handle himself in the rough seas.

Diego wouldn't take the boy, he thought, and he began to ready the boat for the day's expedition.

As if she could read his thoughts, Millie yelped, "Aeaarff!" Her paws reached up at his shoulders, or his heart, Diego couldn't tell.

Millie ran back and forth, first jumping on Diego, then Henry, then Diego. "Aeaarff!" she said, which means "Let's help" in the way dogs named Millie talk.

Diego took another look at the boy, who puffed his chest and threw his shoulders back. Henry took in a deep breath and said, "We have to save my friend!"

Aeaarff!

iego remembered his own skinny legs and strong will. He looked out to the sea and thought about the catch that awaited him.

"You can come," Diego said to Henry. "But this isn't for fun. You'll need to pull in the nets and watch out for Millie."

Millie barked, "Ruuufffff!" which meant she approved, in the way dogs talk.

After the boat was ready, Diego set out to sea – with his skinny dog and a skinny boy – hoping to make a great catch.

Henry sat next to Diego, the rain beating his face, hoping to mend his friend's broken heart.

Millie sat at the front of the boat, not even noticing the rain, ready to see her own friends.

RUUUffff!

nly Millie knew the fun she had as she dove deep into the sea. "Bom dia!" she would say to the sea urchins with their purple, spiky faces poking from the sea bottom. "Olâ eel!" she would say to the green creatures that slithered by. "Steady as she goes!" she'd say to the sea horses with their graceful gait.

The sea creatures loved Millie too. If she struggled with the bulging nets, the turtles came to help, resting the load on their backs to push it to the surface. "Obrigada!" Millie would say to the turtles, which means "Thank you!" in the way turtles talk. As she flipped and turned through the sea grass, the tuna fish would call out, "Enchantee!" which means "Pleasure to see you!" in the way tuna fish talk.

As Diego had predicted, the fish were running. Henry followed Diego's directions. "Pull!" he'd yell, and Henry, with Millie's help, would yank in the nets. The deck was soon full of fish. But Henry couldn't forget his friend, whose cry had now grown into a quiet "Kkruuuuuuuuussshhh."

Obrigada!

Diego was too busy to notice Henry leaning over the side of the boat. Just as Henry had almost touched his friend's back, "Wwwwwwwwooooooosh!" said the wind, and sent a wave crashing against the boat. Diego grabbed at the wheel but the wind pulled the boat sideways. Water poured across the deck, washing Henry into the sea.

"Man overboard!" Diego screamed, and threw Henry the lifeline he kept at the wheel. But the wind was too strong and the line fell far away from Henry.

Diego tried to turn the boat closer, where he could grab Henry by the hand. But the wind was too strong and pushed them further away.

As Henry screamed out, "Diego!" another great wave caught him, pulling him down into the sea.

Diego saw Henry go under, and tried again to turn toward him. But the sea was too rough and the boat wouldn't turn. He looked for Millie, hoping to at least save her. But through the rain, he saw his loyal dog jump off the boat.

Wwwwwooooosh!

"Millie, volta!" Diego screamed. "Come back!" But the dog wouldn't listen. She was in the sea. He watched helplessly as she swam toward Henry, who had found the strength to hold his head above the water.

Henry saw Millie and screamed her name. But then a wave caught her and pulled her down. Henry tried with all his might to swim toward the spot where he had seen her.

Diego didn't know if the dog was strong enough to handle these rough seas. He could see the boy struggling to stay above the surface. He tried again to right the boat.

Millie was under the surface now and she called to her friends. "Olâ!" she said to the eel. "Steady as she goes!" she said to the sea horses with their graceful gait. She called to the turtles, "Ajuda, tartaruga!" which means "Help, turtles!" in the way turtles talk. She called to the tuna and the mackerel and even the Portugese Man o' War. "Ajuda! Ajuda!"

Henry screamed for Millie again. Then he screamed to the sea, "Ajuda, meu amigo!" asking his friend for help.

Diego fought to keep the boat aright. His day's catch had been thrown back into the sea. Just as he was ready to jump into the sea himself, he remembered what the boy said. Couldn't hurt, thought Diego. He stood at the front of the boat and screamed, "Bom dia, mar!" which means "Good morning, sea!" in the way boys talk.

As he said it, Diego heard a sound, "SSSsscccuuuush, sssscccuuuush, ssssscccuuuush, ssssscccuuuush." The waves suddenly stopped crashing. He ran back to the wheel and turned the boat.

Henry heard the sound too. "SSSsscccuuuush, sssscccuuuush, ssssscccuuuush, ssssscccuuuush."

Bom dia, mar!

efore he could say "Bom dia," Henry felt something at his feet. He yanked them back into his chest, afraid. But then he felt himself rise out of the water. He looked down and underneath him was every creature he could ever imagine.

With Millie leading them, the turtles put Henry on their hard backs. Tuna and mackerels swam toward the surface slithering gently under the turtles, helping them carry Henry toward the boat. The sea horses swam nearby, calling, "Steady as she goes!"

Diego had finally steadied the boat. Wiping the rain from his face, he looked for his precious dog and the boy. He couldn't believe his eyes. Henry seemed to be gliding along the sea, a proud prince riding his prized stallion. Millie swam next to him, singing, "Arrruuufff! Arruuufff!" which means "Look at us!" in the way dogs talk.

Behind it all, Diego heard the sea singing good morning, "SSSsscccuuuush, sssscccuuuush, ssssscccuuuush, sssssscccuuuush."

When the boy and the dog reached the boat, Diego lifted them in, shivering and soaked.

"Bom dia!" Diego cried out before pointing the boat toward shore. "Sssssccccuuuuush," said Henry, pretending he was the sea. "Arrrarrrrrarrraaaa," barked Millie, as she thanked her friends.

Just before sunset, Diego pulled the boat into the harbor. He saw two people waiting for them at the shore. Diego wiped his eyes. It can't be, he thought. That looks like the king and queen.

Henry saw the people too and yelled out, "Mother! Father!"

Diego said to Henry, "Son, all that struggling must have confused you. That's the king and queen, not your mother and father."

"The king and queen ARE my mother and father," Henry said.

Diego realized he had never learned the boy's name.

"Are you Henry?" he asked, a chill running up his back.

"Yes, and I didn't eat my breakfast," Henry responded, remembering he had been sent to his room.

Didn't eat breakfast, Diego thought. He had nearly drowned the prince!

When the boat reached the shore, Diego steadied it for Henry, who went running to his parents.

"Henry! What has happened to you?" the queen said.

"My friend stopped crying," said Henry, laughing to himself.

As Diego moved toward the group, the king cried out, "What have you done to my son!"

Henry pulled himself from his mother, who was hugging him, and ran to his father. "Don't be mad, father. I begged him to take me out and the sea stopped crying."

As Henry retold the story of the crying sea and the waves and the turtles, Millie came up beside them. "Ruuufffff!"

"And this dog saved my life!" Henry said.

Reaching the king and queen, Diego bowed. The king just stared.

The queen broke the silence, "If this dog saved your life, she must come to live with us in our castle."

They all looked at the queen. Diego was stunned, but Henry said, "Mother, her name is Milagro, which means miracle in the way fishermen talk. She is a prize water dog. She doesn't belong in the castle. She belongs with the sea."

He took a long breath and continued, "And father, I do not belong in the castle either, I belong with Millie and Diego and my friend, the sea."

The king looked down at the sand, then up again at Diego and his dog, then at Henry.

Henry worried he'd spend the rest of his life in his room.
Diego wondered what the punishment was for drowning a prince.

Finally, the king spoke. "Well, my son, if this is your wish, then from here forth Milagro and all her sons and daughters shall be named the Cãos do Água," which means Portuguese Water Dog in the way kings talk. "They will be protectors of Kings and Fishermen. And Henry, one day, when you have learned the ways of the sea, you too can have your wish."

Forever more, even today, the sons and daughters of Millie protect kings in their castles and fishermen on the shores. They are the patrons of Portugal.

Henry followed his dream and sailed the seas as far as Africa and India. Today he is known as Henry the Navigator. The castle is gone from high on the cliffs of Sagres and in its place sits a school named after Henry, where boys and girls learn to listen to the sea.

Cãos do Água

Henry the Navigator was born in 1394, the son of King João and Queen Philippa. Henry inspired many of the great explorers of history, including Christopher Columbus, Vasco da Gama and Ferdinand Magellan. At his school in Sagres, he taught his students how to listen to the sea and navigate with the stars, and they even built the ship that would take them across the oceans to explore far away lands such as North and South America, India and Africa. They call this time the Age of Discovery or the Age of Exploration.

Milagro's sons and daughters helped fishermen for hundreds of years. The Portuguese Water Dogs would pull in broken fishing nets, herd schools of fish and even carry messages from the owners back to the shore. Today, fishermen use radios and equipment to do their job, but Millie's great, great, great, great-grandson, Bo, still has a very important job; Bo helps the President of the United States of America do his job.

Obrigada!

CPSIA information can be obtained at www.ICGtesting.com
Printed in the USA
BVIW12n0556210517
484630BV00002B/40